PUBLIC LIBRARY
DISTRICT OF COLUMBIA

First published in the United States 1992
by Dial Books for Young Readers
A Division of Penguin Books USA Inc.
375 Hudson Street
New York, New York 10014

Published in Great Britain 1992
by HarperCollins Publishers Ltd
Text copyright © 1992 by Tony Bradman
Illustrations copyright © 1992 by Carol Wright
Printed in
The People's Republic of China
First Edition
1 3 5 7 9 10 8 6 4 2

Library of Congress Cataloging in Publication Data
Bradman, Tony.
It came from outer space / by Tony Bradman;
pictures by Carol Wright. — 1st ed.
p.   cm.
Summary: A visitor from outer space visits
an elementary school class and brings an important
message about physical beauty.
ISBN 0-8037-1098-4
[1. Extraterrestrial beings — Fiction.
2. Beauty, Personal — Fiction.]
I. Wright, Carol (Carol S.), ill. II. Title.
PZ7.B7275It   1992   [E] — dc20   91-17882   CIP   AC

IT CAME FROM OUTER SPACE

by TONY BRADMAN

pictures by CAROL WRIGHT

Dial Books for Young Readers New York

We were all in school,
working hard, when . . .

an alien spaceship
crashed through the roof.
It was quite a surprise!

We were frightened when
the spaceship door
started to open . . .
and we all screamed when
The Monster climbed out.
It was terrifying.

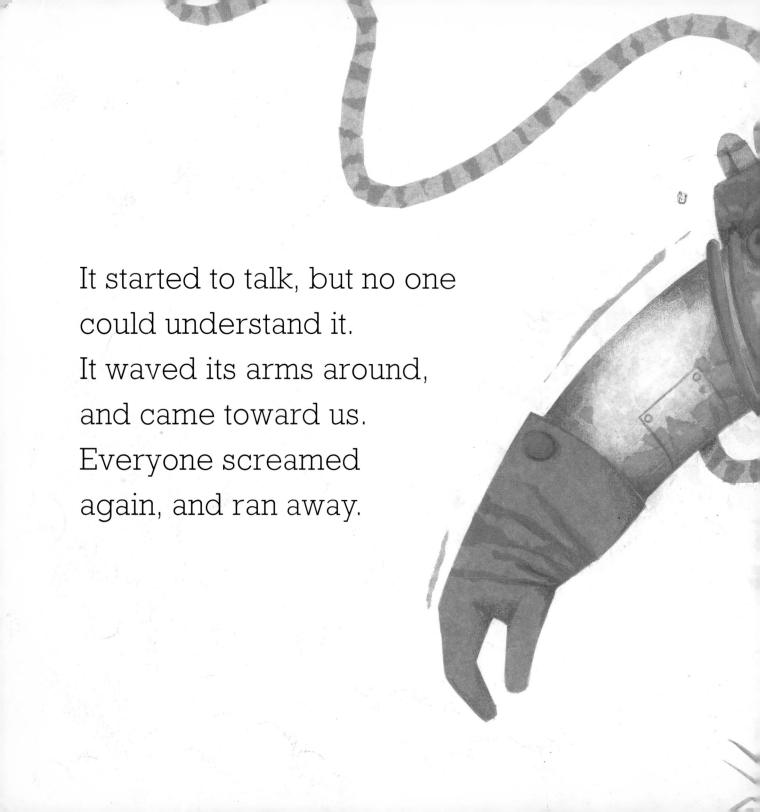

It started to talk, but no one
could understand it.
It waved its arms around,
and came toward us.
Everyone screamed
again, and ran away.

It lumbered after us into the playground.
We were trapped in a corner.

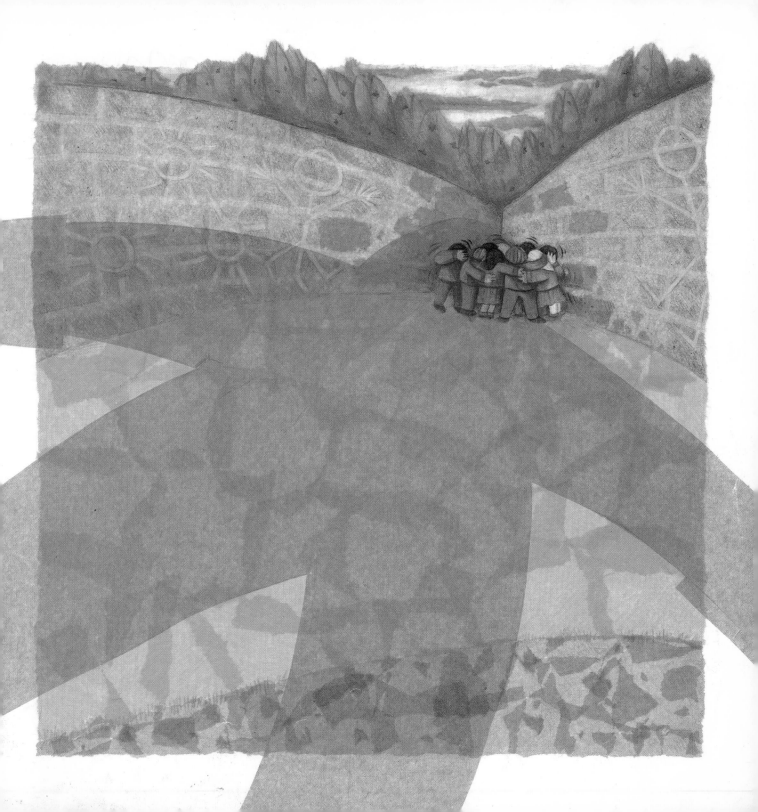

The Monster kept talking
and waving its arms.

And then it took off its helmet.

It was an awful sight.
The Monster's face was
so horrible that we had
to look the other way.

Our teacher fainted.

The Monster turned out to be quite
nice, though. It gave us a present.
It showed us inside its spaceship.
It even showed us some pictures
of its home.

Our teacher, who was feeling better, took a picture of The Monster with her camera.

Then it had to go.

We were sad to see The Monster
fly away. We all waved.
It was a very friendly monster,
even though it was so ugly.
We hope it comes back soon.

At least we've got a picture of
The Monster to remember it by. . . .